uRRmaiDs

3

Seasick Sea Horse

by Sudipta Bardhan-Quallen

illustrations by Vivien Wu

SCHOLASTIC

Scholastic Children's Books
An imprint of Scholastic Ltd
Euston House, 24 Eversholt Street, London, NW1 1DB, UK
Registered office: Westfield Road, Southam, Warwickshire, CV47 0RA
SCHOLASTIC and associated logos are trademarks and/or
registered trademarks of Scholastic Inc.

First published in the United States by Random House Children's Books,
a division of Penguin Random House LLC, New York.
First published in the UK by Scholastic Ltd, 2018

ISBN 978 1407 19258 1

A CIP catalogue record for this book
is available from the British Library.

Printed and bound by CPI Group (UK) Ltd, Croydon, CR0 4YY

Papers used by Scholastic Children's Books are made from
wood grown in sustainable forests.

1 3 5 7 9 10 8 6 4 2

www.scholastic.co.uk

To Heisenberg, Who and Ralf

Shelly stared at herself in the mirror. She was alone in the bedroom she shared with her older sisters, Tempest and Gale. That almost never happened, so Shelly was enjoying it.

Mum poked her head into the room. "Are you ready?" she asked. "Your sisters are still out with Dad. If you hurry, we can eat breakfast together!"

"I'm trying," Shelly replied.

"Hurry up," Mum said.

Shelly grinned. With three kittens in the family, she was constantly sharing with her sisters. They shared a room. They shared toys. And they pretty much always had to share time with Mum and Dad. But today, Shelly had a chance to hang out with her mother with no other purrmaid around.

Unfortunately, Shelly never got ready quickly. She was too picky about the way she looked. She liked having every strand of her white fur in place and every outfit purr-fectly planned. Today, she chose a golden top to go with her starfish clip and her favourite bracelet.

When Shelly twirled her paw, the bracelet sparkled in the light. It always brought a smile to her face. It was beautiful, *and* it matched the ones her best friends, Angel and Coral, wore.

The girls' friendship bracelets had the same three charms: a golden seashell, a gold coin and a lavender pearl. The pearls were the newest additions to their bracelets. They were gifts from the Catfish Club after they all worked on an art project together.

The bracelets looked alike, but Shelly, Angel and Coral were as different as purrmaids could be! Coral was an orange kitten. She was the careful one in their group. Shelly never had to worry about getting her paws too dirty when Coral was in charge. Angel was a black-and-white kitten. She liked to dive headfirst into every adventure. She was fine stretching a rule or two as long as that led to excitement or winning! Shelly liked some rules – but only if she was the one who made them! She didn't always want to admit it, but

Shelly liked getting her way. Together, the three of them made a paw-some team.

When Shelly was finally ready, she heard dishes clinking. "I think I took too long," she grumbled. When she swam into the kitchen, her sisters were already at the table. Tempest was sitting on one side of Mum, and Gale was on the other. "*I* wanted to be next to Mum!" Shelly whined.

"I did, too," Dad said. He gave Shelly a quick kiss on the forehead.

Mum pointed to a spot by Gale. "There's room for you there, Shelly," she purred.

Shelly scowled, but she moved next to her sister.

Dad held up a plate of scrambled tuna eggs. "I made your favourite, Shelly," he said. Both of Shelly's parents were chefs,

but Dad's breakfasts were always fin-tastic. Shelly heard her tummy rumbling. She couldn't wait to eat!

Dad handed the plate to Tempest. She took a big helping of eggs. Mum only scooped a little bit onto her plate. But after Gale took her share, there was hardly any left! "The plate is almost empty," Shelly complained. "You guys took it all!"

"Come on, sis," Gale said. "We weren't taking. *You* were *sharing*!"

"And like Mum and Dad always say, sharing is caring!" Tempest laughed.

Shelly sighed. She loved her family, but it was hard to have to share everything. *It would be nice to have more things that are just mine,* she thought.

Shelly was still frowning as she swam to Leondra's Square to meet Coral and

Angel. But as soon as she saw them, her frown turned upside down. Her best friends always made everything better. "Hello!" she shouted.

Coral spotted Shelly and yelled, "Come on! We're going to be late!"

Shelly laughed. Coral always worried about being on time. They went through the same routine every morning. Even though they'd never missed the school bell.

"We're not going to be late," Shelly said. "Don't worry."

"Let's just hurry," Coral answered.

The girls raced toward sea school. Usually, they swam straight down Canal Street from Leondra's Square to the school doors. But today, something made Shelly stop.

"What are you doing?" Coral asked. "We can't stop!"

Shelly shushed her. "Look at that!" she hissed.

There were two wonderful places on Canal Street. Kittentail Cove Library was on the north side of the street. A fenced-off garden of corals and sea grass called Meow Meadow was on the south side. Shelly pointed at something inside the garden.

Purrmaids often went to Meow Meadow to enjoy the peace and quiet. But today, it was too noisy for anyone to relax. Some purrmaids were fixing the gazebo using planks of driftwood and panels of sea glass. They wore hats that said CASPIAN CONSTRUCTION. It was Mr Caspian and his construction crew.

Shelly wasn't looking at Mr Caspian. She pointed to a purrmaid in the garden. Her rainbow fur was familiar.

"It's Ms Harbour!" Angel shouted.

The gold and silver rings in Ms Harbour's ears and tail glittered as she swam around. A long silver chain hung from one paw.

"It looks like she's searching for something," Shelly said. "Let's go see if we can do anything for her."

As the girls got closer to their teacher, Shelly spied a flash of something light brown hiding in a seaweed hedge.

"What are you doing, Ms Harbour?" Coral asked.

Ms Harbour spun around quickly. "Oh, girls," she gasped. "You surprised me!"

"We're sorry," Angel said. "We just came over to help."

Ms Harbour smiled. "I could use some extra paws!" She pointed to the seaweed

hedge. "I was trying to bring something
special to class today," she explained,
"but he got away!"

Shelly leaned in for a closer look. "It's
a sea horse!" she exclaimed.

"He's adorable," Angel purred.

"I found him this morning when I came to the garden to exercise," Ms Harbour explained. "He was all by himself, and he looked so cute! I made a collar out of an earring and turned one of my necklaces into a leash." She held out the chain. "But as soon as I got the collar on him, he darted away. He's been hiding in this seaweed ever since. What do you think would make him come out?"

Since Shelly's parents were chefs, she knew food could make things better. *Maybe he's hungry*, she thought. She remembered that she had prawn salad in her lunch bag.

"If we're lucky," Shelly said, "sea horses like prawns." She slowly moved toward the sea horse and held out the prawn salad. Then she hovered as still as she could.

The sea horse poked his head out from

his hiding place. He sniffed at the food. Then he swam to the prawn salad and began to eat.

"Quickly!" Shelly whispered. "The leash!"

Ms Harbour carefully attached the leash to the sea horse's collar. "Paw-some job!" she declared. "Thank you, Shelly!"

"Is he your pet?" Angel asked.

Ms Harbour grinned. "Actually, he is going to be our classroom pet."

"I've always wanted a pet!" Shelly exclaimed.

"Well," said Ms Harbour, "now we all have a pet to share." She paused and looked directly at Shelly. "I think Shelly has earned the right to host our pet on his first night with us!"

Ms Harbour led the way to sea school. Shelly grinned from ear to ear. *A pet sea horse for me to take care of!*

"Ms Harbour, can we help Shelly with the class pet?" Coral asked.

"Well, that's Shelly's decision," Ms Harbour answered. "He's her responsibility tonight."

Angel and Coral glanced at their friend. "You'll let us, won't you?" Angel begged.

Shelly bit her lip. She really wanted the sea horse all to herself. But how could she say no to her best friends? "Of course," she said slowly.

Coral and Angel smiled and high-fived.

The four purrmaids arrived outside room Eel-Twelve just as the bell rang. Ms Harbour stopped the girls at the door. She handed Shelly the silver leash. "Hold this," she said. "Wait here until my signal."

Ms Harbour swam into the classroom. "Welcome, class!" she said. "I have something very special to share today!"

"Is it a pop quiz?" Baker asked.

"Or extra homework?" Taylor added.

Shelly covered her mouth as she giggled. Baker and Taylor *really* loved schoolwork!

Ms Harbour laughed. "Not today! But I think you'll like it anyway." She waved to Shelly and her friends. Coral and Angel went in first. Shelly followed them, holding the sea horse's leash. She led him to the centre of the classroom.

"A sea horse!" Umiko shouted. She was one of the purrmaids in the Catfish Club.

Her friends Adrianna and Cascade were the other two girls. Sometimes Shelly and her friends had a hard time getting along with the Catfish Club. But usually, they were all friends.

"Bring him closer!" Cascade said.

Ms Harbour nodded. Shelly led the sea horse up and down the aisles of the classroom.

"He's fin-tastic!" Adrianna purred.

"You all know that the ocean is filled with many different creatures," Ms Harbour said. "Some creatures are harmless." She pointed to the sea horse. "Like Bubbles. He's very friendly."

"Awwww!" Angel said. "Bubbles is a great name!"

Ms Harbour smiled. "Other creatures in the sea can be very dangerous."

"And some creatures look dangerous

but are actually friendly," Coral added. "Like my pal Chomp the catshark!"

"Exactly, Coral!" Ms Harbour laughed. "It is important for purrmaids to learn how to treat the creatures we encounter in our ocean. We have a responsibility to learn how to live with *all* our underwater neighbours. To help with that, I thought it would be nice to get a class pet."

"A class pet!" Baker cheered.

"That's paw-some!" Taylor agreed.

Ms Harbour tied Bubbles's leash to a lamp on her desk and began the lesson. "Many of the animals and plants that live on a coral reef depend on each other," she explained. "Like the yellow tang and the green sea turtle." She held up a picture of a bright yellow fish that Shelly recognized. "Yellow tangs hide in the safety of the reef and eat algae. If there isn't enough food

in the reef, they have to swim somewhere else to look for a meal. But then they could find themselves in danger."

Ms Harbour held up another picture. "Green sea turtles are so big they don't have to worry too much about danger.

Their problem is keeping clean. As they swim through the ocean, they get covered in algae. That makes it hard for them to swim quickly. So they don't like being dirty."

"I know how they feel," Shelly joked. Her classmates laughed. Everyone knew how Shelly liked to stay purr-fectly clean at all times.

"Do you know how these creatures work together?" Ms Harbour asked. "Dozens of little yellow tangs hang out and create a type of cleaning station. Green sea turtles swim through the cleaning station, and the tangs eat the algae on their shells. In the end, the turtles are spotless and the tangs are full!"

Angel asked, "Can purrmaids help clean sea turtles, too?"

Ms Harbour shook her head. "Sea

turtles get nervous around us. If you tried to clean a sea turtle's shell, you'd probably upset him."

"So even though we'd be trying to help," Coral said, "we'd actually be making things worse?"

"Exactly!" Ms Harbour exclaimed. "This is why it's important to learn as much as we can about the ocean around us. We don't want to do harm when we are trying to help."

Ms Harbour continued to teach about other sea creatures. But Shelly had a hard time sitting still. She kept looking at the clock and then over at Bubbles. Shelly wasn't sure, but she thought the sea horse looked a little seasick. *He wants to get out of here, too,* she thought.

Right before the dismissal bell rang, Ms Harbour said, "We didn't have enough time to talk about sea horses today. That will change soon!"

"No, Ms Harbour!" Adrianna moaned.

"Don't give us homework!" Cascade groaned.

"Homework is good for you," Ms Harbour scolded. Then she winked. "I'm just joking. Only one of you will have homework tonight. Every night, someone will have to volunteer to take care of Bubbles at home," she explained. "We can't leave him alone in the classroom, after all."

Shelly grinned. *Finally!* It was time for her to take the pet sea horse home and care for him. She couldn't wait!

"Can I take Bubbles tonight?" Umiko shouted.

"No, I want to!" Cascade yowled.

"My uncle the mayor says I'm very responsible," Adrianna said, "so I would be a good choice to take our class pet home."

Ms Harbour had to hold up a paw to get the class to quiet down. "You'll all get a turn," she said. "But for tonight, I've already chosen Shelly."

"Why?" Baker whined.

"It's not fair!" Taylor complained.

Ms Harbour shook her head. "If it wasn't for Shelly, Bubbles wouldn't even be here right now." She told everyone about what had happened at Meow Meadow. "So I think it's actually very fair to let Shelly have the first turn," she said.

The class nodded. Shelly grinned and said, "I'll take good care of him, I purromise." She zipped out of her seat to get to the sea horse.

"Do you want to stay after class so I can give you some tips about sea horses?" Ms Harbour asked.

Shelly really didn't feel like wasting another second. She just wanted to leave with Bubbles. "I'm all right," she said. "I already know enough, I think." She moved toward the sea horse again.

"If you're sure," Ms Harbour said. "I trust you, Shelly. Take care of him in the best way that you can. Good luck!"

"Don't worry," Angel said. "Coral and I will be there to help Shelly with anything she needs."

"Or anything Bubbles needs," Coral added.

Shelly felt butterfly fish flutter in her tummy. She knew Coral and Angel only wanted to help. *I just want it to be me and Bubbles today,* she thought. This was her chance to have something that didn't have to be shared with anyone. But Angel and Coral looked so excited that Shelly didn't know how to tell them that.

Shelly gulped. *I guess I'll just have to share.*

The three purrmaids and the sea horse slowly swam through Kittentail Cove.

Bubbles followed behind the girls. Shelly had to call back to him a few times to get him to swim.

When they passed Meow Meadow, Shelly felt a tug on the leash. She looked over her shoulder. Bubbles was swimming towards the garden.

"That's the wrong way, silly," Shelly purred. She tugged on the leash.

But Bubbles stopped moving. He dropped to the ocean floor and wrapped his tail around a stalk of bright orange coral. He stared back at Meow Meadow. Shelly thought he looked seasick again.

"What's wrong?" Angel asked. "Why are we stopping?"

Shelly shrugged. "Bubbles doesn't want to swim. I don't know what's wrong."

As they watched, the sea horse started to change colour. He went from tan to

orange – the exact shade of the coral.

"Look! I didn't know sea horses could do that!" Angel gasped.

Shelly was amazed. "That's a neat skill," she said.

"But one that would make it really hard

to find him if he got lost," Coral said.

Shelly leaned down towards Bubbles. She gently unwrapped his tail from the coral and cradled him in her paws. The sea horse changed back to tan. "I wonder what else I'll learn about you tonight," she whispered.

"Well, we can do more learning later,"

Coral said. "We're supposed to be at your house right after school. If we're late, we might get in trouble!"

Shelly and Angel giggled. "Come on, Bubbles," Shelly said. "As soon as we get home, I'm making you a paw-some snack!"

But Bubbles still wouldn't follow! He floated down to the ocean floor again.

"Why won't he swim?" Angel asked.

Shelly scowled. "I don't know," she replied. "Does he look seasick to you?"

"I don't think so," Angel said.

"Maybe this is too far for him to swim," Coral suggested. "I don't know if sea horses are able to swim as far as purrmaids. Do either of you know?"

The girls shook their heads. Now Shelly was

starting to worry. *I hope I actually know enough to take care of him,* she thought. She held Bubbles and gently stroked his head.

Coral thought for a minute. Then she said, "I know! We could just carry him the rest of the way."

"Good idea!" Angel said.

Shelly nodded. It *was* a good idea to carry Bubbles. She just wished she'd thought of it without Coral's help.

Shelly decided not to let that bother her. *I'll still do a great job tonight,* she thought. With Bubbles tucked in her paws, she headed home.

As the purrmaids swam through the front door of Shelly's house, they heard her dad's voice. "Girls," he said, "you're right on time!"

"I was worried about that!" Coral exclaimed. Shelly and Angel laughed.

Then all three girls raced into the kitchen. Because her parents were chefs, Shelly's kitchen was as big as an orca!

"We'll be able to make Bubbles *anything* here!" Coral exclaimed.

"Mum! Dad!" Shelly shouted. "Look at what I have!" She slowly opened her paws to reveal Bubbles.

"Is that a sea horse?" Mum purred.

"This is Bubbles," Shelly answered.

"He's our new class pet," Coral added.

"He's adorable," Mum said. "But taking care of a pet is a big responsibility."

"Are you three going to be able to handle it?" Dad asked.

"Yes—" Angel began.

But Shelly interrupted her. "Actually, it's *my* job to take care of Bubbles tonight."

"And Coral and Angel are here to help?" Mum asked.

Shelly felt those butterfly fish in her tummy again. *I really don't want help,* she thought. "I guess so," she replied.

"Wonderful!" Dad said. "I know the three of you will do a great job taking care of this little guy."

Shelly smiled weakly and said, "Come on. Let's get Bubbles a snack." She found a bowl of prawn and another of sea lettuce. Then she picked up a sea lemon from the counter. "Can you grab some sea cucumbers, Angel?" she asked. "And, Coral, will you get a cauliflower jellyfish?"

"What are you making?" Angel asked.

"My special prawn salad," Shelly replied. "He liked it before. And we can have a snack, too." She hooked the end of Bubbles's leash around a cabinet handle.

"I can chop the cauliflower jellyfish for you," Coral offered.

"And I can slice the sea cucumbers," Angel added.

"I guess that would help," Shelly answered. "Just make sure you cut thin slices and chop small pieces."

Shelly began shredding the sea lettuce. She was used to being in a kitchen with her parents, so she worked quickly. She diced the sea lemon. Then she mixed everything into the bowl of prawn. "I need the other ingredients," she said. She looked at her friends.

Neither Angel nor Coral was ready. Angel had only sliced one sea cucumber. Coral had only finished chopping half the cauliflower jellyfish. But the bigger problem was that they were doing everything *all wrong*!

"Angel!" Shelly snapped. "I said *thin* slices. And, Coral, those aren't *small* pieces! That's not how I make this meal!"

Coral and Angel looked embarrassed.

"I'm sorry!" Coral yelped. "I didn't know I was breaking the rules!"

"We're doing our best," Angel said. "What difference does it make if the pieces are big or small? It will still taste good."

Shelly rolled her eyes. "That's not the way I wanted it," she muttered. "Your help isn't helping!"

Shelly mixed the salad together. She made plates for each of them and a small one for Bubbles. She sighed. "Maybe this won't be so bad."

Shelly tasted the prawn salad. It was different from how she usually made it. But the thicker slices and bigger pieces actually made it taste . . . better.

Shelly did not want to admit that out loud.

Bubbles, though, hadn't even nibbled

at the food. *At least he doesn't like it better their way,* Shelly thought.

The sea horse floated down to the floor. He had the same sad look on his face that he'd had earlier. "Poor Bubbles," Angel said. "I don't think he wanted a snack."

Or maybe we should have done it my *way,* Shelly thought.

Shelly picked up the leash again. "I think I should take him back to Meow Meadow. He seemed to want to go there before. I bet he needs some exercise." She tugged on the silver chain. "Come on, Bubbles," she said.

But just like before, Bubbles didn't move.

Coral and Angel crouched down to get eye to eye with Bubbles. "He just looks so miserable," Angel said.

"Maybe he doesn't want to go for a

swim," Coral suggested. "Could he be
sleepy? Should we try to make him a
bed?"

"Or maybe he wants something
different to eat," Angel said. "What else
do sea horses like?"

Shelly's paw clenched around the leash.
"I really think Bubbles needs to go to the
garden," she repeated. Why weren't her
friends listening?

Suddenly, Coral shouted, "I know!
Let's go to the library and find a book

about sea horses! That way we can figure out what to do to make Bubbles happy!"

"That's a fin-tastic idea!" Angel said. She looked at Shelly, waiting for her to agree.

But Shelly didn't want to go to the library. She didn't want to help Bubbles  sleep or get him a different snack. She wanted to go to Meow Meadow. And she wanted Angel and Coral to just understand that.

Coral reached for the silver chain. But Shelly yanked it away. "Ms Harbour said Bubbles is *my* responsibility," Shelly yelled, "so *I* will decide what to do with him!"

"Calm down," Angel said. "We're only trying to help!" She reached toward Shelly, but her friend moved away.

"Did you ever think that maybe I don't want your help?" Shelly snapped. "That maybe I want to do this *by myself*?"

Both Coral and Angel looked shocked. Their mouths hung open and their eyes grew wide. "We always do stuff together," Coral said. "Like our art project."

"Or exploring that shipwreck," Angel added.

Immediately, Shelly felt bad for saying the things she had. *That stuff didn't sound so mean inside my head,* she thought, *but it's the truth!* She didn't know how to explain it any better. Usually, she loved getting help from her best friends. But this time, she truly did want to take care of the sea horse by herself.

It was completely silent in the kitchen. Angel and Coral looked at Shelly, waiting for her to say something. But Shelly focused on Bubbles so she wouldn't have to say anything.

After a few minutes, Angel grabbed Coral's paw. "Come on, Coral," she said. "Shelly doesn't need our help right now. Let's go to the library. Maybe we can come back later."

Shelly shrugged.

Angel waved. "Bye, Shelly. See you soon," she said. She led Coral out.

"Goodbye," Coral called.

Shelly watched her friends leave. She couldn't help but feel a little excited not to have to share her pet any more. "Finally, it's just you and me, Bubbles," she said. She pulled his leash. "Let's go."

"Are you going out?" Mum called from the other room.

"Yes. Bubbles and I are headed to Meow Meadow," Shelly explained. "He looks a little seasick, and he didn't want to eat the prawn salad we made. I think he needs exercise."

"Where are Coral and Angel?" Mum asked.

Shelly pointed out the window. "They left for the library to read about sea horses."

"I thought they were going to help you with Bubbles," Mum said.

Shelly looked away and played around with Bubbles's leash. She didn't want to tell Mum that she didn't want help from her friends. "Taking care of Bubbles is my job, not theirs," she mumbled.

Mum swam over and began petting the sea horse. "I'm glad that you are taking your responsibility so seriously," she said. "But you should remember that you can be in charge *and* let other purrmaids help you. I know I couldn't handle all the things that need to be done in our restaurant if your father didn't help me." She looked her daughter in the eye. "Like I always say, sharing is caring!"

Shelly scowled. "But I always have to share!" she complained. "At home, I share with Tempest and Gale. At school, I

share with Coral and Angel." She crossed
her paws. "Sometimes I get so sick of
sharing!"

Mum kissed Shelly's forehead. "I can
understand that," she purred. "If you
want to do this job all by yourself, it is
totally your decision. I will support you
no matter what." She kissed her daughter
again. "And I know your best friends

will be on your side no matter what, too. You three have been working and playing together since you were little kittens. I don't think there's anything that could change that."

Now Shelly felt paw-ful. Mum was right. Angel and Coral were good friends. They were already on her side – even when she was telling them to go away.

Shelly knew she had to do something. "I can't just let them leave like this," she said.

Mum smiled. Even Bubbles seemed to nod his head.

"They're my best friends," Shelly said. She grabbed the silver leash. "Let's go, boy. We have to catch up with them."

Shelly hurried down to Canal Street with Bubbles. She paused, then spied her friends way up ahead. Luckily, they were swimming slowly. "If we move fast, we can catch them," Shelly said. She wanted to apologize before the girls got to Kittentail Cove Library. She knew as soon as they were inside, Coral wouldn't let anyone speak. Coral took the QUIET, PLEASE signs very seriously!

Shelly tried to swim forward. The sea horse had a different idea! Shelly felt her paw being pulled to the left. "Bubbles!" she yelped. "What are you doing?"

Bubbles darted into a patch of pink sea sponges. "Come here, boy!" Shelly pleaded. She tugged Bubbles's leash. But he wrapped his tail around a piece of a sponge and turned pink to match it.

"We're not going to be able to hurry like this!" Shelly complained. She scooped the sea horse up.

Shelly and Bubbles reached Coral and Angel just as they were about to open the library door. "Angel! Coral!" she shouted. "Please wait!"

The purrmaids stopped and looked over their shoulders. "What's going on, Shelly?" Coral asked.

Shelly bowed her head. "I needed to

find you two," she said, "to say I'm sorry. I don't know why I said all that stuff. I don't know why I was being so selfish." She sighed. "Can you ever fur-give me?"

Coral and Angel glanced at each other. "I thought you wanted to take care of Bubbles all by yourself," Angel said.

"I did," Shelly replied. "I wanted to be able to do something without having to share any part of it. I feel like I'm always sharing everything – even the things I don't want to share."

"I know how you feel," Coral said. "I don't always like to share with Shrimp. And trust me, one little brother is worse than two big sisters!"

"I hate sharing, too," Angel said.

Shelly rolled her eyes. "You're an only kitten, Angel!" she groaned. "Who do you have to share with?"

Angel shrugged. "I guess nobody," she said. "Maybe that's why I don't like it. I'm not used to it!"

The girls laughed. Shelly felt better

already. She said, "Good thing libraries are built for sharing. Let's go inside and see what we can borrow!"

Coral's smile disappeared. "Shelly," she said, "of course we fur-give you. But you still can't come to the library with us."

Shelly's jaw fell open. "I said I was sorry!" she yowled.

Coral shook her head. "It's not that," she said. She pointed to the library door.

That's when Shelly saw the sign. It said NO PETS ALLOWED.

"You've got Bubbles with you," Coral purred, "and he can't go inside. It's against the rules!"

"We could sneak him inside," Angel suggested.

One look at Coral's horrified face and Shelly knew that wasn't going to happen.

"I guess we can wait out here for you two," she said. She took a seat on the library steps.

"But you'll be bored," Coral said. "I could go inside and ask the librarian if she would give us permission to bring a pet inside. Just this once."

"I have a better idea, Shelly," Angel said. "You wanted to go to Meow Meadow. What if you and Bubbles go to the garden while we check out some books?"

"Then we'll meet you there with anything we find," Coral added. "We all get to do what we wanted and still work as a team."

It was a purr-fect plan!

Shelly hugged her friends. "Bubbles and I will wait for you at the gazebo," she said.

Angel and Coral waved and swam into the library. Shelly turned toward Meow Meadow. The construction crew was gone, so it was much more peaceful than this morning. There was only one purrmaid wearing a construction hat in the garden. It was Mr Caspian. He was swimming around the gazebo, taking notes on his clipboard. He looked like he was checking the repair work.

Bubbles didn't care who was in Meow Meadow. As soon as he saw the garden, he stopped looking even the tiniest bit seasick. He leapt out of Shelly's paws and raced forward, pulling Shelly behind him.

"Whoa, boy!" Shelly said. "I guess you wanted to come to Meow Meadow all along."

Bubbles finally looked happy. *I knew coming here was what he needed,* Shelly thought. He had some bounce in his swimming. "Coral was worried about you not being able to keep up with purrmaids." Shelly laughed. "But I'm the one having trouble keeping up with you!" And she actually *was* getting tired. "Can we just sit down on the steps of the gazebo for a bit?" she asked.

Bubbles didn't want to rest. He tugged at his leash. It was almost like he was searching for something.

Shelly had an idea. "Come here, boy," she purred. When Bubbles came closer, she said, "I'll sit here. You swim around until Angel and Coral get back." She leaned over and unhooked the leash from the sea horse's collar.

Bubbles's eyes widened, like he couldn't believe Shelly was going to let him swim around. He hovered in the water for a moment. And then he was off!

Shelly looked out at Meow Meadow. She waved to Mr Caspian and then looked for Bubbles. She smiled as the sea horse zipped around lightning fast. Just like before, Bubbles changed colours as he moved. When he was in a sea-grass bed, he was green. When he was in a coral patch, he was bright red.

"Shelly!" Coral shouted. She and Angel were swimming through the gates of Meow Meadow.

"Here!" Shelly yowled from the gazebo. She waved to her friends. Then she called for Bubbles. "Come on, boy! Angel and Coral are here!"

Shelly didn't see the sea horse. She swam out to look in some of the sea-grass beds. *Where is he hiding?* she wondered.

Shelly spun all around. Her eyes darted from one side of the garden to the other. But Bubbles wasn't in the sea grass. He wasn't in the coral patches. He wasn't swimming on the garden paths. "Bubbles!" she yelled. "Where are you?"

Shelly felt tears welling in her eyes. *I was supposed to take care of Bubbles,* she thought. *But I lost him!* She sat down on the gazebo steps and stared at the ocean floor.

"We found the purr-fect thing for Bubbles!" Coral shouted. She carried a book with heavy silver corners.

That's when Shelly's tears began to fall.

"Shelly!" Coral said. "What's wrong?"

"Did you really miss us?" Angel joked. "We aren't mad, I promise."

Shelly shook her head. "It's Bubbles," she sobbed. "He's gone!"

"What?" Coral and Angel gasped at the same time.

"He seemed so excited to be here in Meow Meadow," Shelly explained. "I took his leash off so he could really swim around. But then he raced away so quickly! And now I don't know where he went!" She covered her face with her paws. "What if he's gone fur-ever?"

"It's all right, Shelly," Angel soothed. "We'll help you find Bubbles."

"How hard could finding one little sea horse be?" Coral added.

Shelly knew Coral and Angel were trying to help. But finding a tiny creature in a big garden wasn't an easy job. Especially when that creature could change colours to hide!

Shelly squeezed her eyes shut to stop her tears. When she opened them again, she saw Angel and Coral swimming through the garden. Her friends weren't crying like she was. They were looking in clumps of kelp and under starfish. They were searching behind rocks and fences.

They aren't giving up, Shelly thought, *and Bubbles isn't even their responsibility.* She squared her shoulders. *I can't quit, either,* she decided.

Shelly swam over to her friends. "Thanks for helping me," she purred. "What should I do?"

Angel squeezed Shelly's paw and said, "You know we wouldn't leave you all by yourself, right?"

"Bubbles is probably not between here and the library," Coral said. "We would have seen him. So there are only three more directions we need to search."

"I'll take the east side," Angel said.

"I can search the west side," Coral added.

Shelly nodded. "I'll search the south

side," she said. "Remember, Bubbles can change colours. So he might blend in wherever he's hiding."

"We'll look carefully," Angel promised.

"Let's meet back here when we're done," Coral said.

The purrmaids swam off in separate directions. Shelly went straight to a seaweed hedge. *This is just like the one Bubbles was hiding in earlier,* she thought. She examined it carefully. Then she saw something!

"Bubbles?" Shelly yelped. She reached through the seaweed and grabbed . . . a sea slug! "You're not Bubbles," she sighed.

Shelly forced herself to go back to searching. She looked high and low. She turned over every rock and seashell. She found plenty of fish in the sea – but not a single sea horse. *Maybe Angel or Coral has had better luck,* she thought.

Shelly swam back to the gazebo. Coral and Angel were already sitting on the steps. When they saw her, Coral shook her head.

Shelly gulped. "How could this happen?"

"We'll keep looking," Coral said.

Shelly cried again. "We've done everything but take the gazebo apart!" she wailed. "Bubbles is lost fur-ever!"

Coral put a paw around Shelly. "Bubbles isn't lost," she purred. She looked at their other friend. "Angel, you still think we can find him, don't you?"

Angel didn't say anything. She was looking over her shoulder.

"Angel?" Coral called again.

This time, Angel got up from the steps and crouched down next to the gazebo.

Shelly scratched her head. "Is everything all right?" she asked.

Angel popped up. Her smile was dazzling.

"How can you be happy at a time like this?" Shelly said.

"Oh, Shelly!" Angel shouted. "I think I found him! I found Bubbles!" She pointed to the base of the gazebo. "Look!"

Shelly moved closer. "Bubbles!" she said. The sea horse was hovering near a sea-glass panel with his nose poked against the glass.

Shelly leaned down to see what Bubbles was looking at. Behind the sea-glass panel, there was a bright pink finger coral. Something seemed to be clinging to the coral. Shelly squinted to see better. "Sea horses!" she gasped.

There was one sea horse about the same

size as Bubbles. Her tail was wrapped around one of the thickest branches of the coral. And there were many more tiny sea horses trapped behind the wood and glass. They hid in the coral, peeking out at the purrmaid who was staring at them.

The other large sea horse swam up to the sea-glass panel. Soon, she and Bubbles were nose to nose.

Coral grabbed the library book from the gazebo steps. She pawed through the

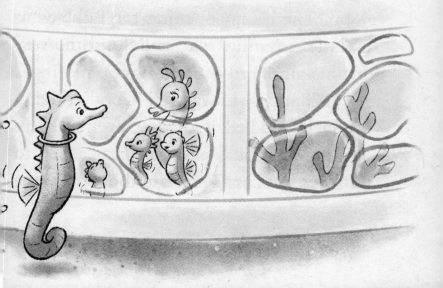

pages and then held the book open for Shelly. "It says here that sea horses like Bubbles take care of their children with their mates," she explained. "They also stay with the same mate for life."

"I think those sea horses are Bubbles's family," Angel said. "That's why he's been sad away from Meow Meadow."

"And why he's been trying to get back to them," Shelly said. "He hasn't been *sea*sick. He's been *home*sick."

Shelly examined the base of the gazebo. The construction crew had done a good job. "There's no opening for Bubbles to get to his family," she said. "And no way for his family to get out."

"What should we do?" Coral asked.

Shelly fiddled with the silver leash in her paw. It could easily be reattached to Bubbles's collar. They could just take the sea horse home and get him ready for sea school tomorrow.

Shelly looked at the sea horse family again. She knew there was only one thing to do. "It's my job to take care of you, Bubbles," she whispered. She scooped him up in her paws.

Bubbles tried to get away from Shelly, but she held him tightly with one paw. With her other paw, she unfastened the sea horse's collar. "You don't belong on a leash," Shelly said. "We need to get you back to your family." She let Bubbles go.

The sea horse stretched his neck now that it was free. Then he did a flip in the water before swimming back to face his mate.

Shelly looked around, trying to find Mr Caspian. Luckily, he was still nearby. "Mr Caspian!" she shouted. "Can you help us?"

Mr Caspian turned and swam towards the girls. "What do you need, Shelly?" he asked.

Shelly pointed to Bubbles. "There's a sea horse family trapped under the gazebo," she explained. "Can you take some of the glass out to free them?"

"Sure thing! The glass panels are designed to break safely if they get hit hard," Mr Caspian said. "If someone was playing ball and accidentally bumped the gazebo, no one would have to worry about cuts from sharp pieces of glass."

"So you *can* help!" Angel exclaimed.

Mr Caspian shook his head. "Actually, I would be able to help," he said, "but I don't have any of my tools with me. I could go back to the office and bring some."

Shelly frowned. "That will take too long," she said.

"Do any of you have something heavy?" Mr Caspian asked. "Something we could use to strike the sea glass?"

"All we have is this library book," Coral moaned.

Shelly gulped. She looked at the book and then at the gazebo. "Can I have the book, Coral?"

"Do you have a plan?" Angel whispered.

Shelly nodded. "Coral might not like it," she said. She took the library book from her friend's paws.

Coral scowled. "What do you mean?" she asked.

"What are the rules about taking care of library books?" Shelly replied.

"Don't rip or fold the pages," Coral began. "Don't lose them. Return them on time."

While Coral rattled off more rules, Shelly swam to one of the sea-glass panels on the gazebo. She gently pushed Bubbles away. Then, in a swift move, she struck the glass with one of the book's metal corners. The glass broke into three

small pieces. Immediately, Bubbles raced through the empty pane and over to his family.

"You did it!" Mr Caspian said.

"It's a purr-fect sea horse door," Shelly said.

"Technically, she didn't even break any rules!" Angel laughed. "After all, the library never said anything about not using books to break glass!"

Coral scratched her head. "I suppose you're right," she said. She bent down to pick up the sea-glass pieces.

"Look at how happy your sea horse friend is now!" Mr Caspian exclaimed.

The three purrmaids swam closer to see the sea horse family all together.

"He's finally home," Shelly purred.

"But how are you going to get him back to sea school?" Angel asked.

Shelly shook her head. "I'm not taking him back," she declared.

"What?" Coral shouted. "Everyone's expecting Bubbles to be our pet! What are you going to tell the class?"

Shelly bit her lip. "I'm going to tell them the truth," she said. "Bubbles is where he belongs."

Shelly knew she had done the right thing by setting Bubbles free. But she was still nervous in the morning. *How can I really tell everyone I let our class pet go?* she thought.

She swam to meet Angel and Coral, holding an empty leash. The other two girls were waiting under Leondra's statue. They were reading Coral's library book.

As soon as Shelly came close, Coral slammed the book shut.

"Let's go," Angel said. "We don't want to be late!"

"*You're* worried about being late?" Shelly asked. That never happened.

"Of course!" Angel replied. "School is really important!"

Coral nodded.

Shelly scowled. Her friends were acting strangely. *Maybe they're worried about telling the class about Bubbles, too,* she thought.

The girls swam quietly to sea school. Shelly felt butterfly fish in her tummy again as she reached Eel-Twelve. She knew she had to tell everyone the truth. But it would be nice to have a little more time before she had to face her classmates.

As soon as the class saw her, they all swarmed around.

"I don't see Bubbles," Baker said.

"Where is he?" Taylor asked.

"Bubbles is—" Shelly began.

But Adrianna interrupted her. "Did you leave him outside?"

Some of the purrmaids went to the door to peek into the hallway. Cascade noticed Shelly fidgeting with Bubbles's leash. "Why isn't he on his leash?" she asked.

"That's a good question," Ms Harbour said. She raised an eyebrow. "Shelly, is there something you need to tell us?"

"I set Bubbles free," Shelly said softly.

Immediately, the students started shouting.

"What?"

"But he was the class pet! You can't decide what to do with him!"

"Did you set him free, or did you lose him?"

"You couldn't even take care of a sea horse for one night!"

Shelly couldn't keep track of who was asking what. But she could tell that her classmates were upset. *And it's all my fault,* she thought. It seemed like everyone was on one side, yelling at her, and Shelly was completely alone.

But then Angel and Coral swam between Shelly and the rest of the class. "Listen up!" Angel yowled. "There are a few things you need to know."

The class quieted down. *What are they doing?* Shelly wondered. She felt as confused as the other students looked.

"Angel and I did some reading," Coral began.

"Actually, Coral did most of the reading." Angel giggled.

"We went to Kittentail Cove Library, and we found a great book about sea horses," Coral continued. "Did you know that sea horse couples stay together for their whole lives?"

Their classmates shook their heads.

"Well, they do," Angel said. "Bubbles has a wife. And children! We found them all in Meow Meadow."

"There were *more* sea horses?" Baker asked.

"Why didn't you bring them all to school?" Taylor added.

"There are some creatures who like living in purrmaid homes and being our pets," Coral explained. "But there are other creatures who want to live free in the wild. Not every animal is meant to be a pet, no matter how much we might love him."

"According to the book, sometimes sea horses make great pets," Angel said. "But Bubbles is different. He has a family. He needs to be with them. That's why Shelly decided to send Bubbles back to his real home."

"Ms Harbour, you told Shelly to take care of Bubbles in the best way she could," Coral said. "That's what she did. She did what was best for Bubbles – even though it meant having to tell all of you that he was gone."

Ms Harbour nodded. "I can see that," she purred. "Taking responsibility for our class pet turned out to be a bigger project than I thought! I agree Shelly did the purr-fect thing. What do you think, class?"

The other students nodded. Shelly blushed. Angel and Coral had explained everything so well that no one was mad any more! *I'm so lucky they're my best friends,* Shelly thought.

"I guess it's better that Bubbles is free," Baker said.

"I just wish we could still see him," Taylor sighed.

Ms Harbour patted the boys' paws. "I know," she agreed. "I wish that, too."

Angel pulled Shelly and Coral aside. "Shelly," she whispered, "we brought Bubbles back to his home, right?"

"I think so," Shelly answered.

Coral flipped the book open again. She pointed and said, "It says sea horses are very possessive of their homes. Once they find a place they like, they don't want to leave."

"If that spot under the gazebo is home for Bubbles and his whole family," Angel said, "then they should still be there in Meow Meadow."

"And we can see them there," Shelly said. "Ms Harbour!" she called. "Can we go on a field trip? I want to show you all where Bubbles lives."

Shelly led the way to Meow Meadow. When the class reached the edge of the garden, she said, "We need to be very quiet, especially as we get closer to the gazebo. We don't want to scare away any sea horses."

"Do you really think Bubbles is still here?" Baker asked.

"What if he's not?" Taylor asked.

"Coral read that sea horses stay in the same home if they can," Shelly replied.

"And if Coral did the research, I trust her facts!" Angel laughed.

Coral grinned. Shelly smiled, too, but she also motioned for everyone to be quiet. "The gazebo is just up ahead," she whispered. She pointed to the one broken panel of sea glass. "That's the door we made for Bubbles. Let's get closer. Maybe the sea horse family will be home."

The purrmaids slowly followed Shelly toward the gazebo. But before they got there, something darted out at Shelly. "Eek!" she shrieked. The something swam right into her.

It wasn't a some*thing*. It was a some*one*. "Bubbles!" Shelly shouted. "It's you!"

"He recognizes you," Ms Harbour said.

Bubbles nuzzled Shelly's cheek. Then he swam back to the gazebo. Shelly motioned for the other purrmaids to follow the sea horse.

Bubbles swam through the opening under the gazebo and disappeared for a moment. Then he came out – this time with dozens of baby sea horses!

"I think Bubbles is introducing us!" Shelly laughed.

The sea horses swarmed around the purrmaids. They seemed to be as curious about their visitors as the class was about them!

"Look at all of them!" Baker squealed.

"They're beautiful!" Taylor said.

"I'm very impressed," Ms Harbour said. She put a paw on Shelly's shoulder. "I knew I could count on you to take care of Bubbles," she said. "I just didn't realize how

creative you'd be! You treated Bubbles with
kindness and respect. I'm proud of you."

Shelly blushed. "Bubbles can still be
our class pet," she suggested, "even if he
doesn't live in our classroom."

Umiko asked, "Can we visit Bubbles here, Ms Harbour?"

Ms Harbour shrugged. "Why not? Meow Meadow is for everyone in Kittentail Cove."

"So we can still care for our pet and his family," Shelly declared. "We'll share our sea horses with the whole town!"

"That is a fin-tastic idea!" Cascade said.

"And as my uncle the mayor always says," Adrianna added, "sharing is caring!"

"My parents say that, too!" Shelly laughed.

Shelly's classmates clapped. Angel and Coral cheered the loudest. *I really did do what is best for Bubbles,* Shelly thought.

As everyone crowded near the gazebo to play with Bubbles and his family, Shelly floated away. She wanted to let her friends get a good look.

Coral and Angel swam over to where Shelly hovered. They were both grinning from ear to ear. "We have a surprise for you," Coral said.

Angel held something out in her paw. "Coral cleaned up the sea glass yesterday so there wouldn't be a mess in the garden," she said. "When she went to throw the pieces away, I thought they were just so purr-ty."

"Angel had the idea to make them into charms for our bracelets!" Coral squealed. "There were three pieces, and so we were able to make three charMs"

"Now we'll have reminders of Bubbles wherever we go," Angel said.

Shelly took the sea-glass charm from Angel. It sparkled in the light. "This is beautiful," she said. "Thank you so much. And not just for the charm! Thank you for helping me take care of Bubbles, and for explaining to the class what I did. I couldn't have done this all by myself."

Angel and Coral hugged their friend.

"What are friends for?" Coral said.

"We're here for you," Angel purred.

Shelly smiled and said, "I can't wait to share more paw-some adventures with the two best friends any purrmaid could have!"

Don't miss
the next adventure!

PuRRmaids 4

Search for the Mermicorn

Sudipta Bardhan-Quallen

"This is my favourite ocean animal." Angel pointed at the drawing with one paw. "My project will be about mermicorns!"

She was expecting her friends to be as excited as she was. But Shelly looked surprised, and Coral looked confused.

"What do you think?" Angel asked.

Shelly wrinkled her nose. "I guess it's a good idea," she answered.

Coral said, "I think Ms Harbour wants us to pick a *real* animal for the project."

"Mermicorns *are* real!" Angel squealed.

Coral bit her lip. "Have you ever seen one?" she asked.

Angel scowled. "No," she replied. "But that doesn't mean they don't exist. I've never seen a human, either. And I know they're real!"

Shelly giggled, but Coral frowned. "Even though *you've* never seen a human, other purrmaids have," she said. "I don't know anyone who has seen a mermicorn."

Angel looked down at the mermicorn drawing. The creature had the head and body of a horse, with a rainbow mane. She had a tail that looked like a fish's with rainbow scales, and she had a pearly horn on her head. Angel didn't want to think that something so beautiful was just make-believe. "Shouldn't we believe in things even if we can't see them?" she asked quietly.

8/10/18

Francesco Quaglia

Sudipta Bardhan-Quallen

has never met a mermaid, but she did have three cats in college. She is the author of many books for young readers, including *Duck, Duck, Moose!*; *Chicks Run Wild*; *Hampire*; and *Snoring Beauty*. She lives in New Jersey with her family and an imaginary pony named Penny. Visit her online at sudipta.com.

Vivien Wu

has illustrated several books with Random House and Disney Publishing, including five Little Golden Books. She also has an online shop, where she creates more artwork populated by purrmaids and feline-folk. She lives in Los Angeles with her cat, Mimi. Visit her online at vivienwu.com.